JANE BRESKIN ZALBEN

Mousterpiece

A NEAL PORTER BOOK

ROARING BROOK PRESS

NEW YORK

For their enthusiasm and input, a big thank you goes to Neal Porter, Elizabeth Harding, Steven Zalben, and to Susan Hayden, for her special red mouse!

Published by Roaring Brook Press
Roaring Brook Press is a division of Holtzbrinck Publishing Holdings Limited Partnership
175 Fifth Avenue, New York, New York 10010
mackids.com

Library of Congress Cataloging-in-Publication Data

Zalben, Jane Breskin.
    Mousterpiece / Jane Breskin Zalben.
        p. cm.
    "A Neal Porter Book."
    Summary: Janson the mouse, who lives in a museum, becomes an acclaimed
artist by copying the styles of paintings she sees there. Includes notes
about the artists and works featured.
    ISBN 978-1-59643-549-0
    [1. Artists—Fiction. 2. Mice—Fiction. 3. Art museums—Fiction. 4.
Museums—Fiction.] I. Title.
    PZ7.Z254Mou 2012
    [E]—dc23
                                                              2011021755

Roaring Brook Press books are available for special promotions and premiums.
For details contact: Director of Special Markets, Holtzbrinck Publishers.

First edition 2012
Book design by Jennifer Browne
Printed in China by Toppan Leefung Printing Co. Ltd., Dongguan City, Guangdong Province

1   3   5   7   9   8   6   4   2

For my mother who took me for art lessons at the Metropolitan Museum of Art,

and in memory of my father who called my paintings "love pictures."

Janson lived in a museum, tucked into the corner
of a room filled with beautiful old furniture.

Each night after the museum closed
she loved to explore in the dark,

until, one night, she came to a place
she had never seen before . . .

and her little world opened.

She began to draw pictures like
the ones she saw on the walls.

Janson painted in dots,

squares, circles, triangles,

squiggles and wiggles

and stripes.

She cut bright flat shapes

bursting with bold colors.

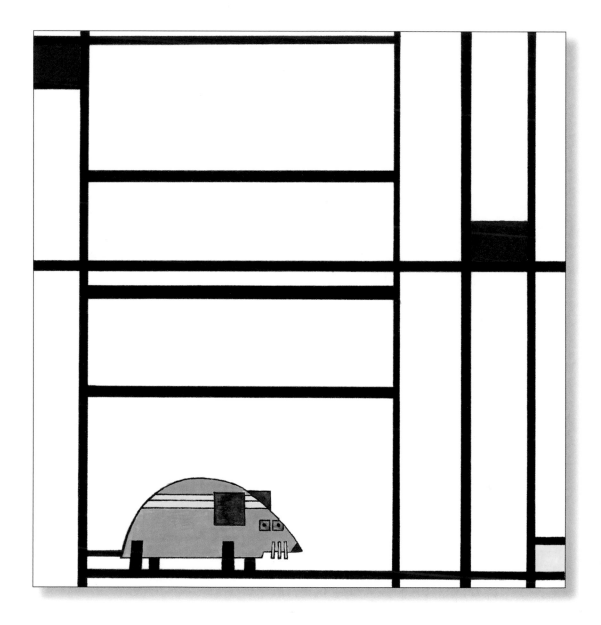

She painted inside the lines,

and then outside them, dripping paint everywhere.

She put her face on a soup can

and tried sculpture.

Then, one night, she saw a big sign:

MODERN WING
CLOSED FOR
RENOVATION

All the walls were bare,
and she could no longer visit
any of her favorite paintings.

So Janson worked on her pictures
and left them in an empty room each night,

until one by one the walls were filled with art.
The more she painted, the happier she became.

One day, the head of museum saw them and said,
"Whose work is this?"

Janson whispered in the tiniest voice,
"Mine."
"Absolutely brilliant!
We must give you an exhibition,"
said the museum director.

People came from far and wide to see
the work of the budding artist.
Some loved it.
Others didn't.

But the last picture was Janson's very best.
It made her happier than anything she had painted.
It was . . . *a mousterpiece.*

Because she did it
her own way.
In her own style.
Unlike anyone else's.

And that is when
Janson knew she
had become a true artist.

31

I named my heroine Janson in honor of
H. W. Janson whose *History of Art*
was "the Bible" we used when I was an art
student in college. We had to memorize each
image in the book, which covered prehistoric
art to the mid-twentieth century. The question
we continuously asked ourselves was,
"Why is this art?"

Janson's Favorite Artists

Page 9: Josef Albers (1888–1976). An artist who both studied and taught at the Bauhaus. His studies utilized flat painted squares of color. He did hundreds of paintings and prints in a series begun in 1949, *Homage to the Square.*

Page 10: Henri Rousseau (1844–1910). A self-taught French painter best known for his fairytale-like jungles and wild animals as demonstrated in his most celebrated work, *The Dream* (1910).

Pages 11 and 20: Andy Warhol (1930–1987). One of the founding fathers of the pop art movement, famous for his 1960s Campbell's Soup Can paintings and silkscreen portraits of the actress Marilyn Monroe and other celebrities.

Page 12: Georges Seurat (1859–1891). A French artist associated with pointillism, in which dots of color applied to the canvas give the optical illusion of blended hues when seen from a distance.

Page 13: Georges Braque (1882–1963). A French artist who, along with Picasso, is credited with inventing cubism in 1908. Through multiple perspectives, different sides of an object could be seen at once.

Page 13: Pablo Picasso (1881–1973). A Spanish painter considered *the* leading figure of twentieth century art whose work incorporated many styles, including cubism, surrealism, and neoclassicism.

Page 13: Marcel Duchamp (1887–1968). A French artist associated with the dadaist movement. Famous for his cubist painting *Nude Descending a Staircase*, he later created sculptures from common found objects, paving the way for the installation art we see today.

Page 14: Paul Klee (1879–1940). A Swiss artist whose playful use of shapes in nature and his interest in music were expressed through multicolored squares, triangles, and rectangles.

Page 14: Wassily Kandinsky (1866–1944). A Russian painter credited with the first work of abstract (non-representational) art, as demonstrated in his floating pastel forms and lines.

Page 14: Joan Miró (1893–1983). A Spanish artist most often associated with cubism and surrealism, whose work often used fluid, amoeba-like shapes.

Page 15: Frank Stella (1936–). An American painter associated with minimalism, who, in the 1960s, created shaped canvases of Day-Glo colors arranged in straight or curved lines, separated by pinstripes of unpainted canvas.

Page 17: Henri Matisse (1869–1954). A French master who, early in his career, was associated with the Fauves ("wild beasts"), who used bright colors, wavy lines, primitive patterns, and negative space. Late in life he created collages using hand-cut shapes of painted paper. His piece *Icarus* inspired the art on this page.

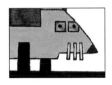

Page 18: Piet Mondrian (1872–1944). A Dutch artist famous for his geometric compositions of black and white rectangles, primary colors (red, yellow, and blue), and thick, straight, black lines.

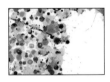

Page 19: Jackson Pollack (1912–1956). An American abstract expressionist whose illustrious "drip" paintings were spontaneously splattered across canvas on his studio floor.

Page 21: Claes Oldenburg (1929–). A Swedish-born artist whose enormous sculptures of everyday objects such as clothespins, hamburgers, and geometric mice (!) are found in many public art spaces and parks.

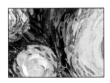

Page 24: Vincent van Gogh (1853–1890). A Dutch post-impressionist whose renowned painting, *The Starry Night* (1889), incorporated broad, swirling brushstrokes, and is referenced here.

Page 24: Salvador Dali (1904–1989). A Spanish surrealist who paired dream-like images together, with objects floating or melting over landscapes, creating avant-garde art.

 Page 25: Chuck Close (1940–). An American artist who starts with a grid and by painting small lozenges of color creates paintings that are perceived from a distance as a single, cohesive image.

 Page 25: Edvard Munch (1863–1944). Norwegian symbolist painter whose most famous work, *The Scream* (1893), is referenced here.

 Page 26: Roy Lichtenstein (1923–1997). An American pop artist who based his imagery on comic strips and cartoons, utilizing black outlines, captions, a screen of primary-colored dots, and stripes patterned over a white background.

 Page 27: Mark Rothko (1903–1970). An American abstract expressionist whose mature work features huge rectangles of two or more lush colors on a background.

 Page 27: Robert Motherwell (1915–1991). An American abstract expressionist who, in the 1950s, paired colors of the Spanish flag with black bars and ovals on white stripes in his Elegy to the Spanish Republic series.